Mr. Bump

Written and Illustrated by
Adam Hargreaves

MR MEN AND LITTLE MISS™
& © 2000 Mrs Roger Hargreaves. Printed and published in 2000
under licence from Price Stern Sloan Inc., Los Angeles.

Published in Great Britain by Egmont World Limited,
a division of Egmont Holding Limited,
Deanway Technology Centre, Wilmslow Road, Handforth,
Cheshire SK9 3FB, UK.

Printed in Italy

ISBN 0 7498 4892 8

Mr. Bump was regretting his choice
of a desert-themed garden.

Mr. Silly

"Dry rot, rising damp, subsidence, leaky plumbing, woodworm, burst pipes, wet rot, death watch beetle, cracked plaster, loose tiles ... I think I'll go and live in a tent."

Plumbing is best
left to the professionals.

Mr. Clumsy

Mr. Wrong's roof garden didn't work as well as he'd hoped it would.

Mr. Happy regretted
asking Mr. Small
to hang his pictures.

Mr. Forgetful knew there was something he should have remembered before he laid his new carpet.

Mr. Worry always suffered from a stiff neck after a visit to Mr. Bump's house.

Little Miss Scatterbrain's confusion over metric and imperial measurements produced some surprising results.

Mr. Messy found that
each time he used his extension
cable it never reached quite as far
as it had the last time.

It was difficult to tell exactly what Mr. Messy had intended to paint after he had finished painting.

Mr. Worry's shelf,
though not a thing of beauty,
was guaranteed never to fall down.

Little Miss Sunshine has a thing about skylights.

Mr. Wrong has the ability to make the easiest tasks look difficult.

Mr. Mean could see no reason in the world why he should spend good money buying a bench from a garden centre when he could make his own.

Mr. Nonsense was really chuffed with his new railway sleeper decking.

A good workman always blames his tools.

Mr. Grumpy

"No, he was putting up a shelf this weekend."

Mr. Nonsense had a sneaking suspicion that he had been somewhat over ambitious with his garden pond.

When she got it home, Little Miss Dotty was not very impressed with her flat-pack wardrobe.

SAFETY FIRST

Mr. Worry

Mr. Wrong

Little Miss Splendid
liked to keep one
step ahead of
the Jones's.

Little Miss Dotty's paint effect was not
what Mr. Happy had had in mind.

Mr. Muddle was forever painting himself into a corner.

Mr. Mean had read that building a conservatory would add value to his home.

Mr. Topsy-Turvy's cat was
more agile than most.

When it came to bricklaying, Mr. Silly was particularly good at pointing.

Mr. Mean's furniture is not so much distressed as just plain distressing.

Little Miss Dotty was very pleased with her new wood flooring.

Mr. Silly's friends couldn't help but

Mr. Uppity's welcome mat
wasn't all that welcoming.

Mr. Dizzy's evening classes in 'How To Change A Light Bulb' were not very well attended.

Mr. Sneeze

Choice of decor can reveal a lot about someone's personality.

"There is nothing ... cough ...
like a real ... cough ... log fire ... cough
... absolutely nothing."

Mr. Silly plastered over the cracks before decorating.

Everyone had been so complimentary about the magazine rack he'd made in his school woodwork class, he felt few qualms about fitting his new kitchen.

Mr. Daydream